For Daniel Barnard,
who listened to me telling stories
on October 13, 2008
S.G.

For Jamie
J.B.

ORCHARD BOOKS
338 Euston Road, London NW1 3BH
Orchard Books Australia
Hachette Children's Books
Level 17/207 Kent Street, Sydney NSW 2000

First published by Orchard Books in 2009
First paperback publication in 2010

Text © Sally Grindley 2009
Illustrations © Jo Brown 2009

The rights of Sally Grindley to be identified as the author and
Jo Brown to be identified as the illustrator of this work
have been asserted by them in accordance with the
Copyright, Designs and Patents Act, 1988.

A CIP catalogue record for this book is available from the British Library.
All rights reserved.

ISBN 978 1 84616 152 0 (hardback)
ISBN 978 1 84616 160 5 (paperback)

1 3 5 7 9 10 8 6 4 2 (hardback)
1 3 5 7 9 10 8 6 4 2 (paperback)

Printed in China

Orchard Books is a division of Hachette Children's Books,
an Hachette UK company.

www.hachette.co.uk

THE BEAR DETECTIVES

Bucket Rescue

Written by **SALLY GRINDLEY**
Illustrated by **JO BROWN**

ORCHARD BOOKS

Constable Tiggs

Sergeant Bumble

Little George

Freddie

One morning, Sergeant
Bumble and Constable Tiggs
were cleaning their car.

A young bear ran up to them.
"Come quickly, Sergeant
Bumble," he cried. "My brother
has fallen down a hole!"

"Fallen down a hole!" said
Bumble. "That is serious."
"Very serious," said
Constable Tiggs.

"Don't worry, Little George,
we'll soon have him out,"
said Bumble.

They jumped into the car with
Little George, turned on
the siren and drove
to the hole.

"Help me, help me!" a voice
cried from down below.
Bumble and Tiggs
stared into
the hole.

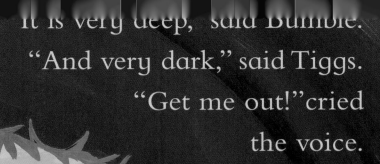

"It is very deep," said Bumble.
"And very dark," said Tiggs.
"Get me out!"cried
the voice.

"Don't worry,
young Freddie, we'll
soon have you out,"
called Sergeant Bumble.

"What we need is a long rope," said Tiggs.

"Excellent idea," said Bumble.

"Where can we find one?"

"Barney the builder will
have one," said Tiggs.
"That's just what I was thinking,"
said Bumble. "You go and fetch it
while I take charge here."
Tiggs zoomed off in the car.

A large crowd gathered to see what was happening. "Stand back," ordered Bumble. "We don't want anyone else to fall in."

"I'm frightened!" cried Freddie.

"Help is on the way," said Bumble.

13

Tiggs arrived with a long piece of rope.

"Well done, Constable Tiggs," said Bumble. "Now, young Freddie, we're going to lower a rope into the hole and we want you to grab it."

"It might be best if you tie it round your waist," called Tiggs. "That's just what I was going to say," said Bumble.

They lowered the rope into
the hole. Everyone held the
other end, ready to pull.

"Have you got it yet?"
called Bumble.

"I can't tie it,"
cried Freddie.
"My paws are too cold."

"Perhaps we could tie the rope
to a bucket and lower the bucket
down the hole," suggested Tiggs.

"That's just what I was thinking,"
said Bumble. "You go and find a
bucket while I stay in charge here."
Tiggs zoomed off
again in the car.

"When we lower the bucket down, you must climb into it and then we will pull you back up," Bumble called down the hole.

"I'm frightened," said Freddie. "There's no need to be frightened when Sergeant Bumble is here," said Bumble.

Tiggs arrived back with a large yellow bucket. They tied the rope around the handle and lowered it down the hole.

"Climb into
the bucket
and hold
on tight,"
called
Bumble.

"I'm in the
bucket,"
cried Freddie.

"Pull,
everybody,
pull!" ordered
Bumble.

They all pulled as hard as they
could. At last, the bucket reached
the top of the hole, and Freddie
fell out onto the ground.

Everybody clapped, and George
gave his brother a big hug.

"Are you all right, young fellow?"
asked Tiggs.

"All right?" said Freddie. "That was
fun! Can we do it again, please?"

Bumble looked at him
in astonishment.

"No, I'm afraid not," he said.
"Holes are dangerous, and buckets
are for fetching water. Off you
go home now, and be careful not
to play near any more holes."

"OK, Sergeant Bumble," said
Freddie and George.

"And now, Constable Tiggs,
I think it's time we went back
to the police station for
a nice bucket of tea."

THE BEAR DETECTIVES

SALLY GRINDLEY 🤠 JO BROWN

Bucket Rescue	978 1 84616 152 0
Who Shouted Boo?	978 1 84616 109 4
The Ghost Train	978 1 84616 153 7
Treasure Hunt	978 1 84616 108 7
The Mysterious Earth	978 1 84616 155 1
The Strange Pawprint	978 1 84616 156 8
The Missing Spaghetti	978 1 84616 157 5
A Very Important Day	978 1 84616 154 4

All priced at £8.99

Orchard Colour Crunchies are available from all good bookshops,
or can be ordered direct from the publisher:
Orchard Books, PO BOX 29, Douglas IM99 1BQ
Credit card orders please telephone 01624 836000
or fax 01624 837033 or visit our website: www.orchardbooks.co.uk
or e-mail: bookshop@enterprise.net for details.

To order please quote title, author and ISBN
and your full name and address.
Cheques and postal orders should be made payable to 'Bookpost plc.'
Postage and packing is FREE within the UK
(overseas customers should add £2.00 per book).

Prices and availability are subject to change.